Bugs

Hide and Seek

By Laura Buller

LONDON, NEW YORK,
MELBOURNE, MUNICH, and DELHI

DK UK
Senior Editor Deborah Lock
Project Art Editor Ann Cannings
Producers, Pre-production
Francesca Wardell, Vikki Nousiainen

Reading Consultant Shirley Bickler

DK Delhi
Editor Nandini Gupta
Art Editor Jyotsna Julka
DTP Designer Anita Yadav
Picture Researcher Aditya Katyal
Deputy Managing Editor
Soma B. Chowdhury

First published in Great Britain by
Dorling Kindersley Limited
80 Strand, London, WC2R 0RL

The publisher would like to thank the following for their kind permission
to reproduce their photographs:
(Key: a-above; b-below/bottom; c-centre; f-far; l-left; r-right; t-top)

1 Fotolia: Eric Isselee (clb). **4 Alamy Images:** Maximilian Weinzierl (c). **Dreamstime.com:** Kaarsten
(c/torn paper). **5 Dorling Kindersley:** Jerry Young (t). **7 Dreamstime.com:** Kaarsten (tr/torn paper).
Getty Images: Art Wolfe (tr). **8 Dreamstime.com:** Kaarsten (bl/torn paper). **9 Corbis:** Frank Lane Picture
Agency / Ron Austing (bc). **10–11 Dreamstime.com:** Gines Valera Marin (border). **10 Jerry Young:** (bl).
12–13 Corbis: Ch'ien Lee (b). **14–15 Alamy Images:** Ernie Janes. **16–17 Dreamstime.com:** Gines Valera
Marin (border). **The Natural History Museum, London:** (c). **17 The Natural History Museum, London:**
(bc). **19 Alamy Images:** Fotofeeling / Westend61 GmbH. **20 Corbis:** SHOSEI (b). **22 Corbis:** Design Pics /
Philip Rosenberg (ca); Bernard Radvaner (b). **22–23 Dreamstime.com:** Gines Valera Marin (border).
23 Corbis: John Lund (b); National Geographic Society / John Cancalosi (tl).
28–29 Corbis: Minden Pictures / Mark Moffett. **30–31 Alamy Images:** Gian Luca Dedola.
32–33 Dreamstime.com: Gines Valera Marin (border). **Getty Images:** skeeg (tombstone).
32 Dorling Kindersley: The Natural History Museum, London (tc, c). **34 Alamy Images:** FLPA (t).
35 Science Photo Library: Dr Morley Read (b). **36 Alamy Images:** Carrie Garcia (t). **37 Dreamstime.com:**
Kaarsten (tc/torn paper). **39 Dreamstime.com:** Kaarsten (clb/torn paper). **40–41 Dreamstime.com:** Gines
Valera Marin (border). **40 Corbis:** Minden Pictures / Piotr Naskrecki (bc). **41 Corbis:** Minden Pictures /
Thomas Marent (cla). **Pearson Asset Library:** Pearson Education Ltd / Malcolm Harris (clb)
Jacket images: Back: Corbis: Minden Pictures / Mark Moffett cla;
Spine: Corbis: Visuals Unlimited / Gary Meszaros

All other images © Dorling Kindersley Limited
For further information see: www.dkimages.com

Discover more at
www.dk.com

Contents

Pssssst!

Hey, you!

Yes, you – the reader.

Can you spot me?

Look up close.

Do you see me yet?

I know what you are thinking.

Where am I hiding?
All you can see is
a tree branch.
Maybe I will hop down.
You are in for a big surprise!
Are you ready?

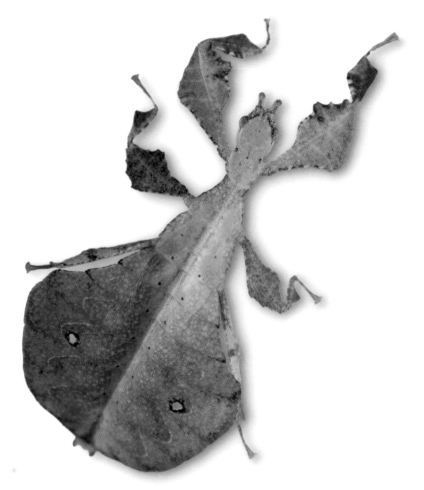

Ta dah!

Here I am.

Are you surprised?

I am not a leaf
fallen from the tree.
I am a bug.
I am called a walking leaf.
(Cool, right?)
My body looks just like
a real leaf.
That is how I can hide
in the trees.
I even move like a leaf.
I shake back and forth
like a leaf in the wind.

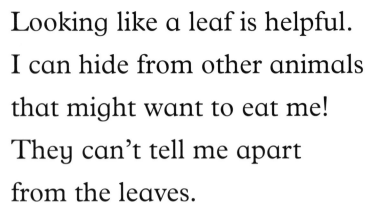

Looking like a leaf is helpful.
I can hide from other animals
that might want to eat me!
They can't tell me apart
from the leaves.
So, they leave me alone!
I am not the only bug
that is good at hiding.

There are many bugs that
use this trick.
Would you like to meet
the others?
I warn you, some are very
hard to spot!
Let's look for them.

Camouflage

animal's skin pattern
that makes the animal
hard to see in its
surroundings

Praying
mantis

African
toad

Gaboon
viper

11

Take a Look!

Can you spot anything
along the branch?
The branch is home
to a very clever bug.
Do you see it yet?

Look carefully
at the green twig.
It seems to have six legs!
A pair of long antennae
stretches from its head.
That is not a twig.
It is a stick insect.

The stick insect's body
is the same shape as a twig.
It is the same colour, too.
A stick insect can stay
very still for ages.
It hides in the tree
all day long.

At night, the stick insect
hunts for food to eat.
It nibbles on tree leaves.
No one can spot it
in the darkness.

By morning, the stick
insect is hiding again.
Let's not stick around!

Introducing **the World's**
Longest
Stick Insect

6 long legs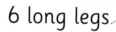

Length: nearly 57 cm (22 in.)
Habitat: rainforests in Malaysia
Discovered: 2008

Chan's megastick

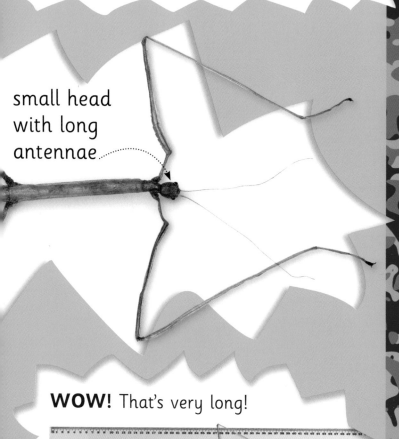

small head
with long
antennae

WOW! That's very long!

Some plants are very green,
but there is much
more to be seen!
Look at this blade of grass.
Can you see a bright
green grasshopper?
The grasshopper is exactly
the same colour as its home.
It blends in so well,
no one can spot it –
apart from you, that is!
Now, let's get hopping.

Look at this tree.
Its bark is so wrinkly
and brown.
This is not a good hiding
place for a bug.
Or is it?

Aha!

There is a cicada [si-KAH-da]
hiding right on the tree.
Its colours match the bark
so well.
Birds like to eat these bugs.
The cicada stays very still
until the bird flies past.

Hide-and-seek
Animals

Jackson chameleon is as green as the forest.

Scorpion fish is as spiky and colourful as coral.

Lantern fly has a head that looks like an alligator.

Tiger has stripes that look like the tree trunks.

Some bugs can only
stay alive if they can hide.
Do you want to
really test your
bug-spotting skills?

Let me show you
some more hidden bugs.
(Sometimes even I can't
find them!)
Now I think I can
with your help.

Be Careful!

Do not prick your finger
on that thorny branch.
Those thorns look sharp.

Wait a second!
Those are not thorns.
They are treehoppers.
These bugs poke holes in
branches and feed on sap.
They can hide
and snack!
That is clever.

What do you see here?
A pile of rocks!
Maybe there is a bug
hiding there?

Hang on!

One of those rocks just moved.

I saw it with my own eyes!

That, my friend, is a rock bug.

A rock bug sits

as still as stone.

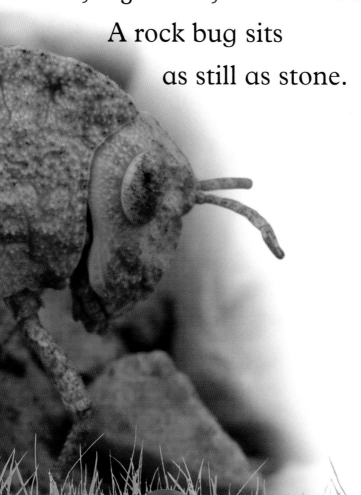

What do we have here?
Something has landed
in the sand.
It is a grasshopper.
Its body colours match
the sandy grains.

Imagine you are a bird
flying over the beach.
Could you spot that bug
in the sand?
I do not think so.
You would keep flying, and
miss out on your beach picnic.

Insects that Play Dead

This leaf butterfly looks like two dead leaves.

The comma butterfly has old, ragged wings.

This stick insect has a wrinkled body.

This leaf mantis is shaped like a dead leaf.

33

What a strange-looking
bug we have here!
It is a spiny katydid.
This creature lives
in the rainforests.

Those thorns on its body
help it to hide in the forest.
Bats like to eat katydids,
but all those thorns can
scare them away.
(They are scaring me, too!)

I see a snake. Do you?

Hang on!

There is something odd
about that snake.

It is really a caterpillar,
playing a cool trick.

First it pulls in its legs.
Then it blows up
the front part of its body
like a balloon.
Spots on its underside look
just like snake's eyes.
Any bird who sees it
is ssssscared.

Just a Minute!

That bug reminds me
of someone.
Someone very close to me.
Someone who looks as if
it fell out of my family tree.

Bingo!

It's another leaf insect,
like me.
It's time for us to leave you.
We are off to a new
hiding place.
I wonder if you will
spot us there?
We will see you.
Will you see us?
Keep looking!

Bug Look-alikes

Some bugs look like other bugs. Why? This is a clever way to sneak up on prey or put off their enemies from eating them.

Ant

Jumping spider
(eats ants)

Wasp
(has a sting)

Hoverfly

Ladybird
(has a bad smell)

Ladybird
mimic spider

Bugs Word Search

Some bugs look like other things. Can you find these six hidden words?

bark   leaf   rock
sand   thorn   twig

t	h	o	r	n
w	s	r	o	b
i	l	n	c	a
g	e	g	k	r
s	a	n	d	k
k	f	e	a	d

Bugs Quiz

1. What is the name of the world's longest stick insect?

2. What is the word for an animal's skin pattern that helps it to hide?

3. What are cicadas hiding from?

4. What do treehoppers look like?

5. What insect does a hoverfly look like?

Answers on page 45.

Glossary

antennae pair of moving parts on the head of an insect that picks up touch and taste

bark covering of the trunk of a tree or bush

chameleon lizard that is able to change its colour

habitat place where animals and plants live

rainforest thick forest where it rains a lot

thorn sharp point on the stem of some plants

Index

Word Search

t	h	o	r	n
w	s	r	o	b
i	l	n	c	a
g	e	g	k	r
s	a	n	d	k
k	f	e	a	d

Answers to the Bugs Quiz:

1. Chan's megastick;

2. Camouflage;

3. Birds; 4. Thorns;

5. Wasp.

Guide for Parents

DK Reads is a three-level interactive reading adventure series for children, developing the habit of reading widely for both pleasure and information. These chapter books have an exciting main narrative interspersed with a range of reading genres to suit your child's reading ability, as required by the National Curriculum. Each book is designed to develop your child's reading skills, fluency, grammar awareness, and comprehension in order to build confidence and engagement when reading.

Ready for a *Beginning to Read* book

YOUR CHILD SHOULD

- be using phonics, including consonant blends, such as bl, gl and sm, to read unfamiliar words; and common word endings, such as plurals, ing, ed and ly.

- be using the storyline, illustrations and the grammar of a sentence to check and correct his/her own reading.

- be pausing briefly at commas, and for longer at full stops; and altering his/her expression to respond to question, exclamation and speech marks.

A VALUABLE AND SHARED READING EXPERIENCE

For many children, reading requires much effort but adult participation can make this both fun and easier. So here are a few tips on how to use this book with your child.

TIP 1 Check out the contents together before your child begins:

- read the text about the book on the back cover.

- read through and discuss the contents page together to heighten your child's interest and expectation.

- make use of unfamiliar or difficult words on the page in a brief discussion.

- chat about the non-fiction reading features used in the book, such as headings, captions, recipes, lists or charts.

46

TIP 2 Support your child as he/she reads the story pages:

- give the book to your child to read and turn the pages.

- where necessary, encourage your child to break a word into syllables, sound out each one and then flow the syllables together. Ask him/her to reread the sentence to check the meaning.

- when there's a question mark or an exclamation mark, encourage your child to vary his/her voice as he/she reads the sentence. Demonstrate how to do this if it is helpful.

TIP 3 Praise, share and chat:

- the factual pages tend to be more difficult than the story pages, and are designed to be shared with your child.

- ask questions about the text and the meaning of the words used. These help to develop comprehension skills and awareness of the language used.

A FEW ADDITIONAL TIPS

- Try and read together everyday. Little and often is best. These books are divided into manageable chapters for one reading session. However after 10 minutes, only keep going if your child wants to read on.

- Always encourage your child to have a go at reading difficult words by themselves. Praise any self-corrections, for example, "I like the way you sounded out that word and then changed the way you said it, to make sense."

- Read other books of different types to your child just for enjoyment and information.

Series consultant **Shirley Bickler** is a longtime advocate of carefully crafted, enthralling texts for young readers. Her LIFT initiative for infant teaching was the model for the National Literacy Strategy Literacy Hour, and she is co-author of *Book Bands for Guided Reading* published by Reading Recovery based at the Institute of Education.

Here are some other
DK Reads you might enjoy.

Pirate Attack!
Come and join Captain Blackbeard and his pirate crew
for an action-packed adventure on the high seas.

Deadly Dinosaurs
Roar! Thud! Meet Rexy, Sid, Deano and Sonia
the dinosaurs that come alive at night in the museum.
Who do you think is the deadliest?

Playful Puppy
Holly's dream has come true – she's given her very own
puppy. Although she tries to train him, share her
delight in the playfulness of her new puppy.

Little Dolphin
Follow Little Dolphin's adventures when he leaves
his mother and joins the older dolphins for the first
time. Will he be strong enough to keep up?

Mega Machines
Hard hats on! The mega machines are very busy
building a new school. Watch them in action!

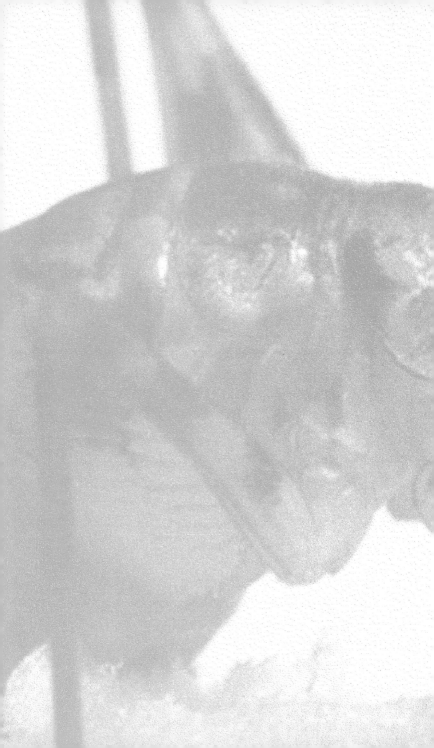